To order additional copies of this book, contact:
Xlibris
844-714-8691
www.Xlibris.com
Orders@Xlibris.com

ISBN: Softcover   978-1-6641-8734-4
        EBook   978-1-6641-8733-7

Print information available on the last page

Rev. date: 07/27/2021

PREVIOUSLY ON

JURASSIC SENTRIES

After a civil war breaks out on the planet Saurna and causes it to become uninhabitable. The Sentries send five of their young to Earth to defend it from the arriving Conquers. Now fifteen yesrs have past the young Sentries have grown and the Cretaceous Conquers have arrived. Will these new Jurassic Sentries be able to defend the Earth as planned?...

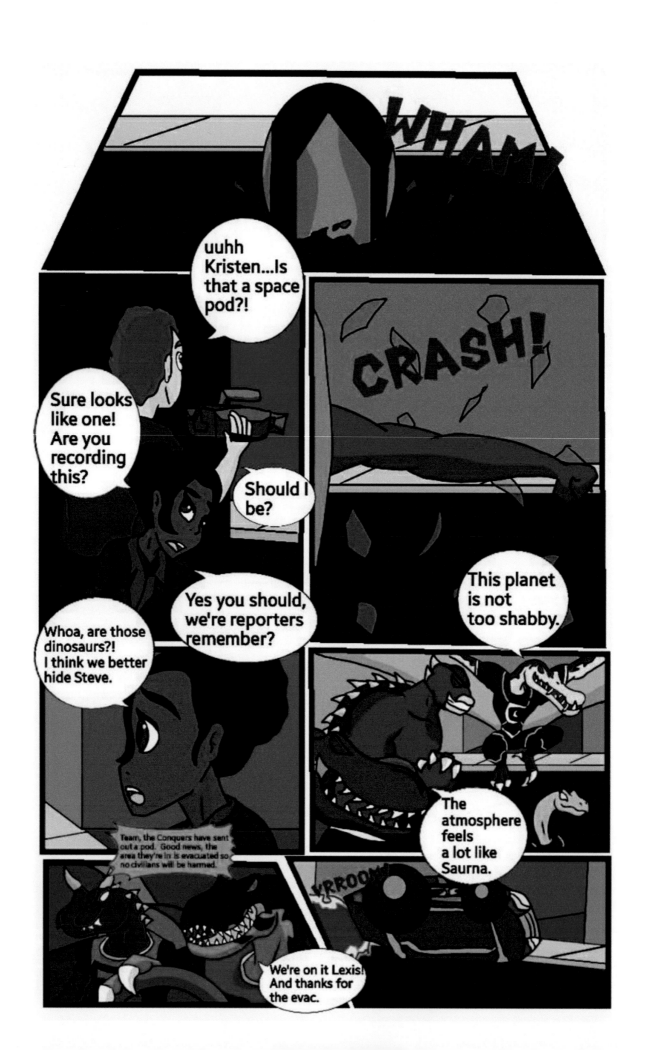

They've arrived.

There! That's where the signal's coming from!

Oh dang!

What's that commotion? Am I here already?

Hey let me go!

You're going to Spinus now!

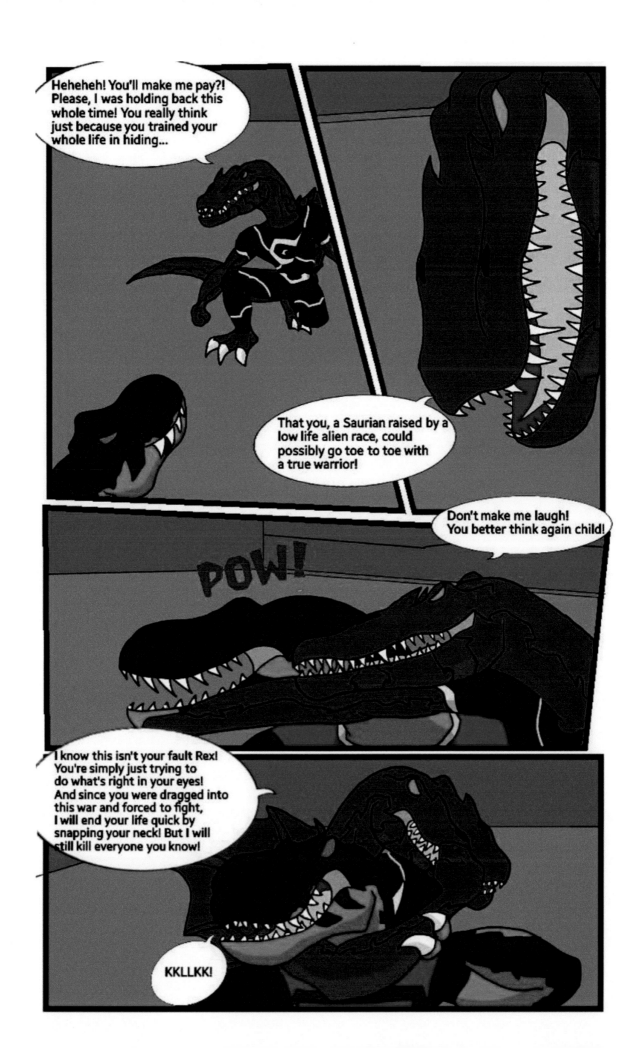

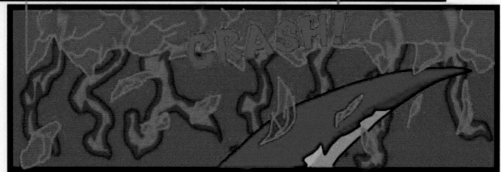

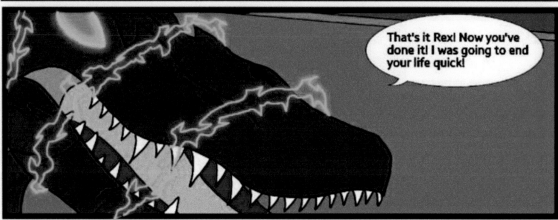

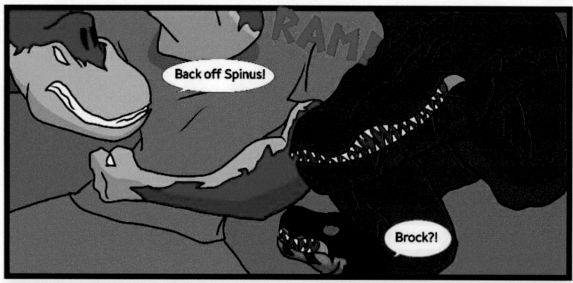

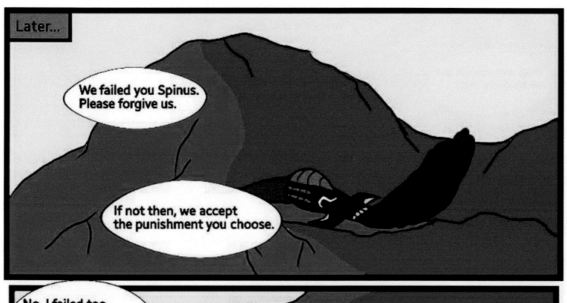

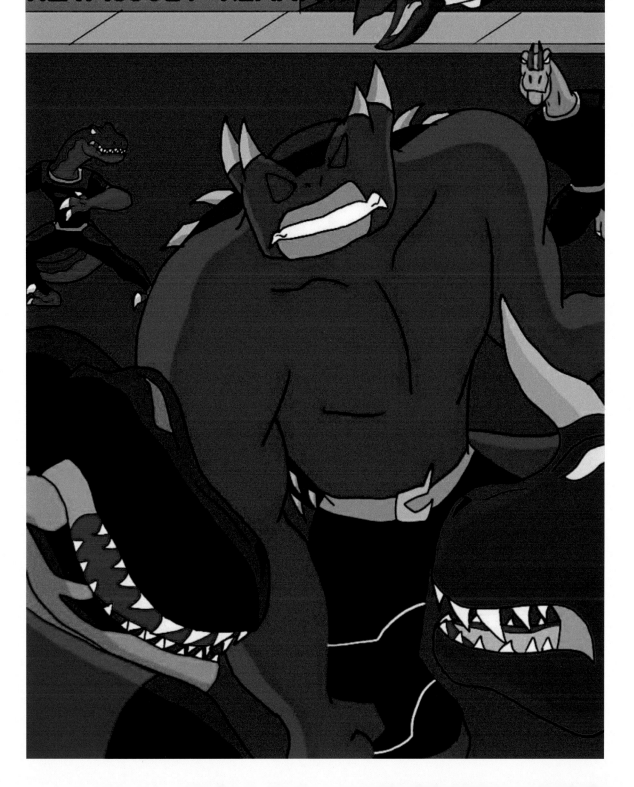

Printed in the United States
by Baker & Taylor Publisher Services